P9-CEY-549

Aggie the Brave

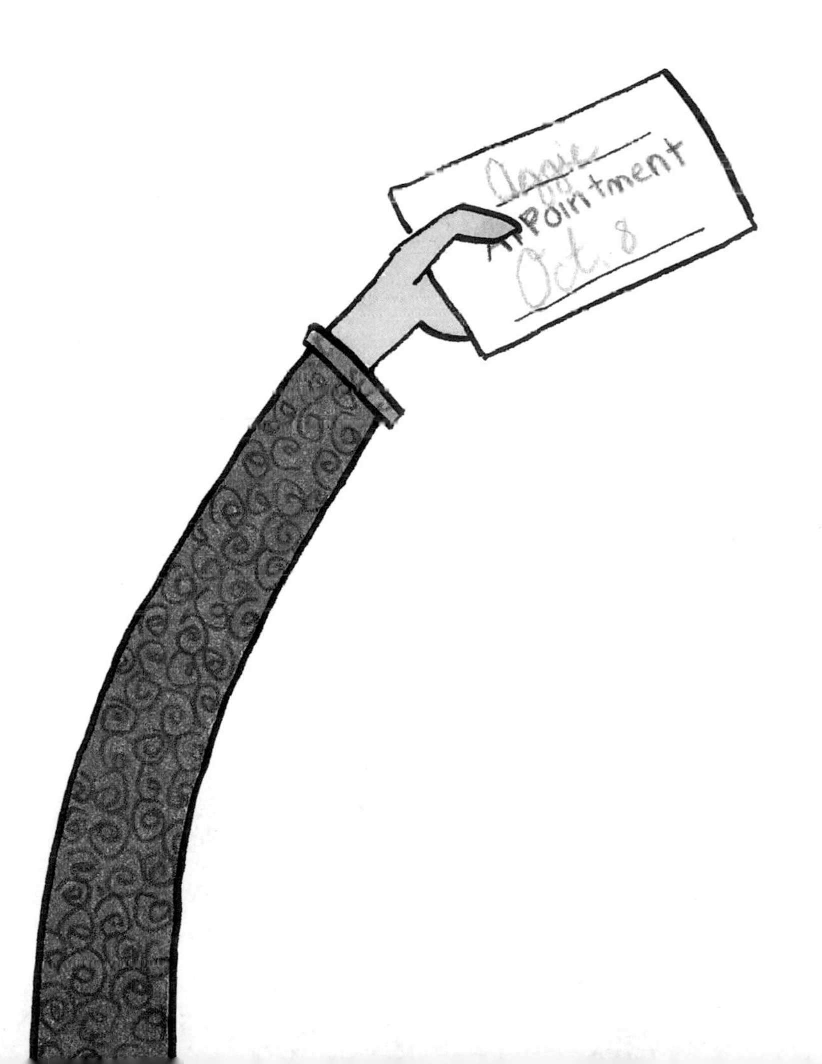

Aggie the Brave

Lori Ries

***Illustrated by* Frank W. Dormer**

Charlesbridge

With love to David, Daniel, Jennifer, Katie, and Ross. Special thanks to Dr. Michelle Taylor and the Sorrento Animal Hospital for keeping Pupster's sight and limbs strong—L. R.

For Teddy, and the amazing staff at the Guilford Veterinary Hospital—F. W. D.

Published by Charlesbridge
85 Main Street
Watertown, MA 02472
(617) 926-0329
www.charlesbridge.com

Library of Congress Cataloging-in-Publication Data
Ries, Lori.
Aggie the brave / Lori Ries ; illustrated by Frank W. Dormer.
p. cm.
Summary: Although Ben is worried about his dog Aggie when the veterinarian spays her and while she recovers, he laughs at her problems with the cone she must wear on her head until her stitches are removed.
ISBN 978-1-57091-635-9 (reinforced for library use)
[1. Dogs—Fiction. 2. Spaying—Fiction. 3. Veterinary medicine—Fiction.]
I. Dormer, Frank W., ill II. Title.
PZ7.R429Agm 2010
[E]—dc22 2009026646

Printed in Singapore
(hc) 10 9 8 7 6 5 4 3 2 1

Illustrations done in pen and ink and watercolor on 140-lb. cold-press Winsor and Newton paper
Display type set in Tabitha and text type set in Janson
Color separations by Chroma Graphics
Printed and bound February 2010 by Imago in Singapore
Production supervision by Brian G. Walker
Designed by Susan Mallory Sherman

A Visit to the Vet

Aggie is going to the vet.
A vet is a doctor for animals.
Aggie is going to the vet to get spayed.

Mommy says this is a good thing to do.
It will keep Aggie from getting sick
when she gets older.
And it means she won't have any puppies.

I know all about doctors.
I am a very good patient.
I am always brave.

Aggie is nervous. She tries to hide.
"No, Aggie," I say. "Be brave!"

She tries to run away.
“No, Aggie!” I say.

I see something silly.
"That dog has a lamp shade
around its head!" I say.
"It is a collar," Mommy says, "a special collar
that keeps dogs from scratching."

“You do not want a silly collar
like that, Aggie!” I say.
“Ruff!” Aggie agrees.

It is our turn now.
I am full of questions.
Will Aggie get hurt?

What if she gets hungry?
Can I wait here for her?

The vet tells me Aggie will sleep.
She tells me Aggie will not feel anything.
"Aggie might not feel hungry when
she gets home," she says.

I do not like what she tells me next.

She tells me I can pick up Aggie tomorrow.

It is hard to leave Aggie.
"You will be okay," I tell her.
"Be good for the vet, Aggie. Be a good dog."
"Ruff!" Aggie says.

“We’ll take good care of Aggie,” the vet says. “I will call you when we are done with the surgery.”

“Be good, Aggie! Be brave!” I say.

It is a long drive home.

I do not feel so brave now.

The Long Day

It is a long day without Aggie.
She is not here to play.
She is not here to read.

The phone rings.
I jump up. Mommy nods.
"Hello?" I say.
"The surgery is over," the vet says.
"Aggie did well. She is resting."
"Thank you!" I say.

I put on my pajamas.

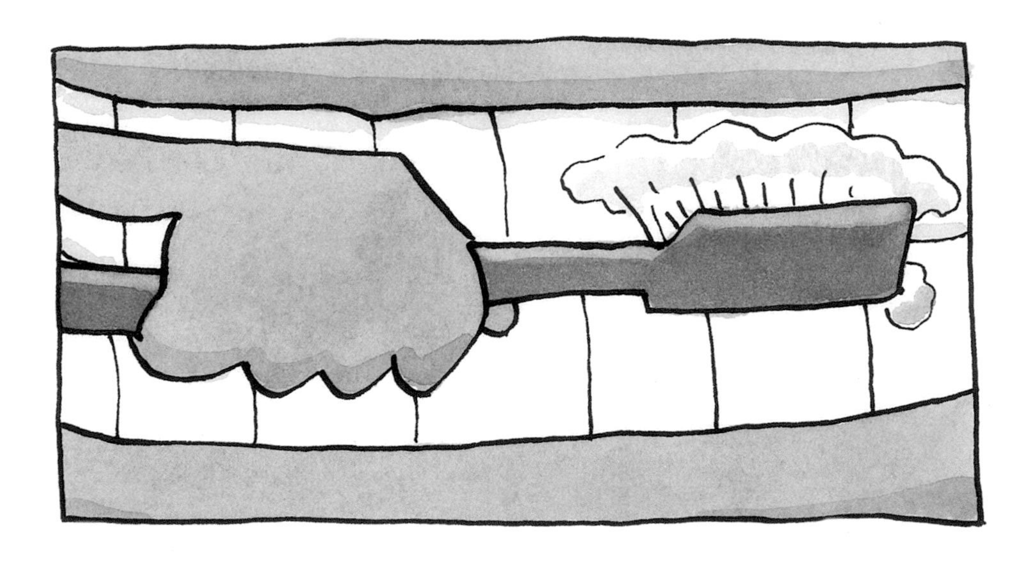

I brush my teeth.

I climb into bed.
"But it's only four o'clock," Mommy says.
I smile big.
"If I go to sleep, then tomorrow will come.
Tomorrow, Aggie will come home."

“Let’s make popcorn,” Mommy says.
She picks a movie from the shelf.

It is a good one—but my lap is empty.

My bed is empty, too.
I miss Aggie.
I know Aggie misses me.
She has never had a sleepover before.

Finally tomorrow comes.
It is time to go to the vet.

I can't wait to see Aggie.

She will run and jump.

She will circle my legs.

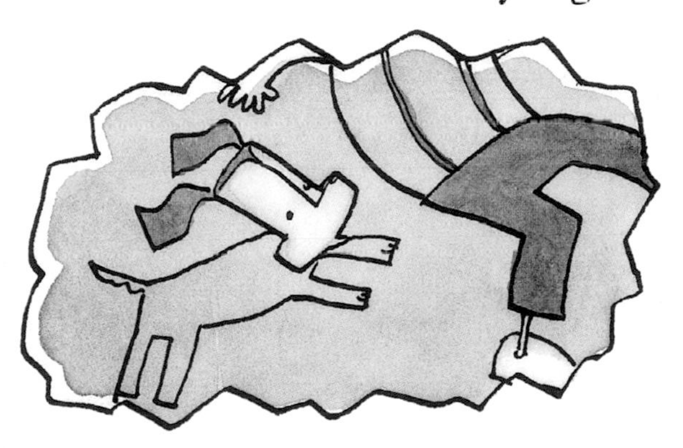

She will play chase.

But when we get to the vet,
Aggie does not play.
Aggie just lies down.
She is lying down with a big
lamp shade on her head.

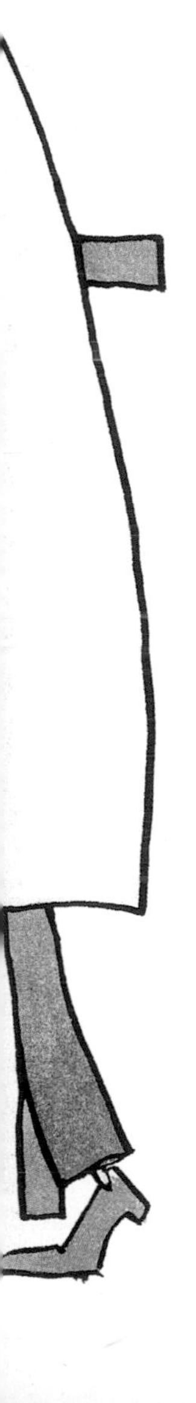

"Aggie will have to be quiet," the vet says.
"She has stitches."
Aggie cannot run.
She cannot play.
She must rest.
"Bring her back in two weeks, and I will
take the stitches out," says the vet.

At home, Aggie looks sad.
"I am sorry you have to be a lamp-head,
Aggie," I say.
"But you have stitches.
You cannot scratch.
You cannot lick.
And you cannot bite your stitches."
"Hmph," Aggie says.
Two weeks is a really long time.

Get Well Soon

The next morning,
Aggie looks better.
She gets up.
She walks around.

Thunk! goes her lamp head.

Whoosh! goes her cone head.

"Owoooo!" goes Aggie the Clown.

Poor Aggie.
She is embarrassed.
"I will rest with you, Aggie," I say.
I get my fancy crayons.

Aggie whines while I color.
I pat her head.
I get an idea.

"Oh! You are NOT a lamp head, Aggie!"
I grab my brown crayon.

"You are NOT a cone head!"
I work and work.
"You are NOT a clown. You are a . . .

LION!"

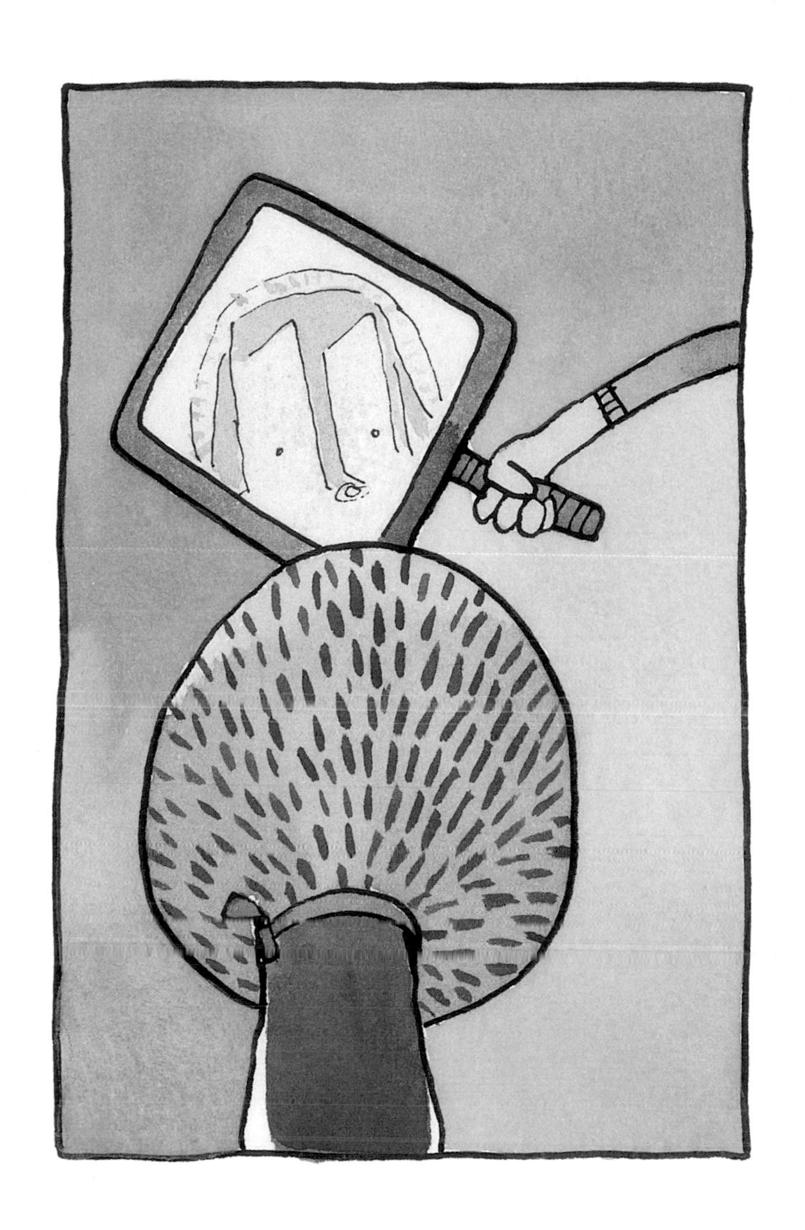

I show Aggie the lion.
"Ruff! Arf! Arf!"
My lion-dog sits tall.

Every day, Aggie feels
a little bit better.

Her lion head helps.

Finally it is time to go back to the vet.

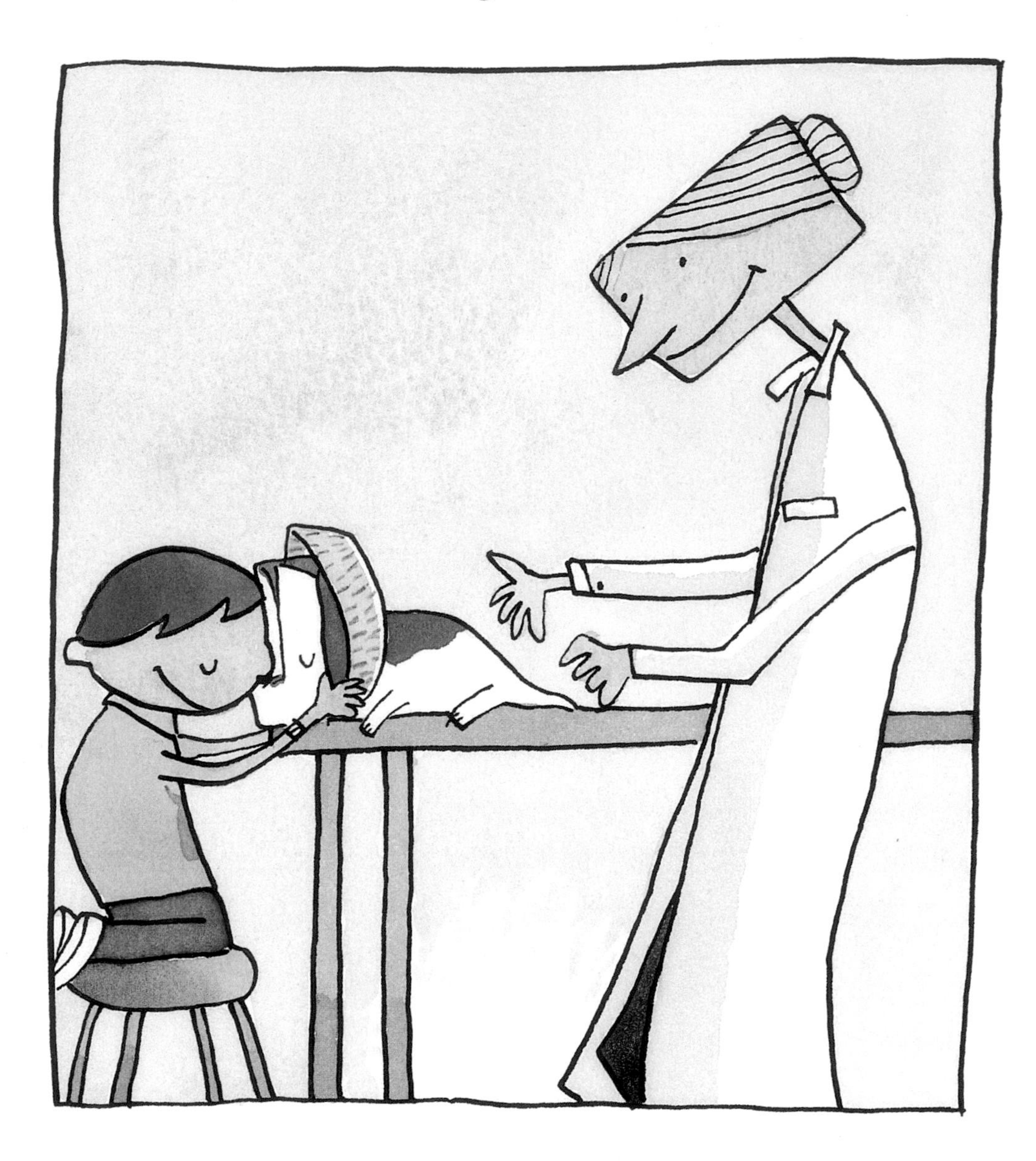

The stitches go away.
"Aggie has healed well," the vet says.

The vet gives her a meaty treat—
a meaty treat for a brave lion.
Aggie loses her mane.

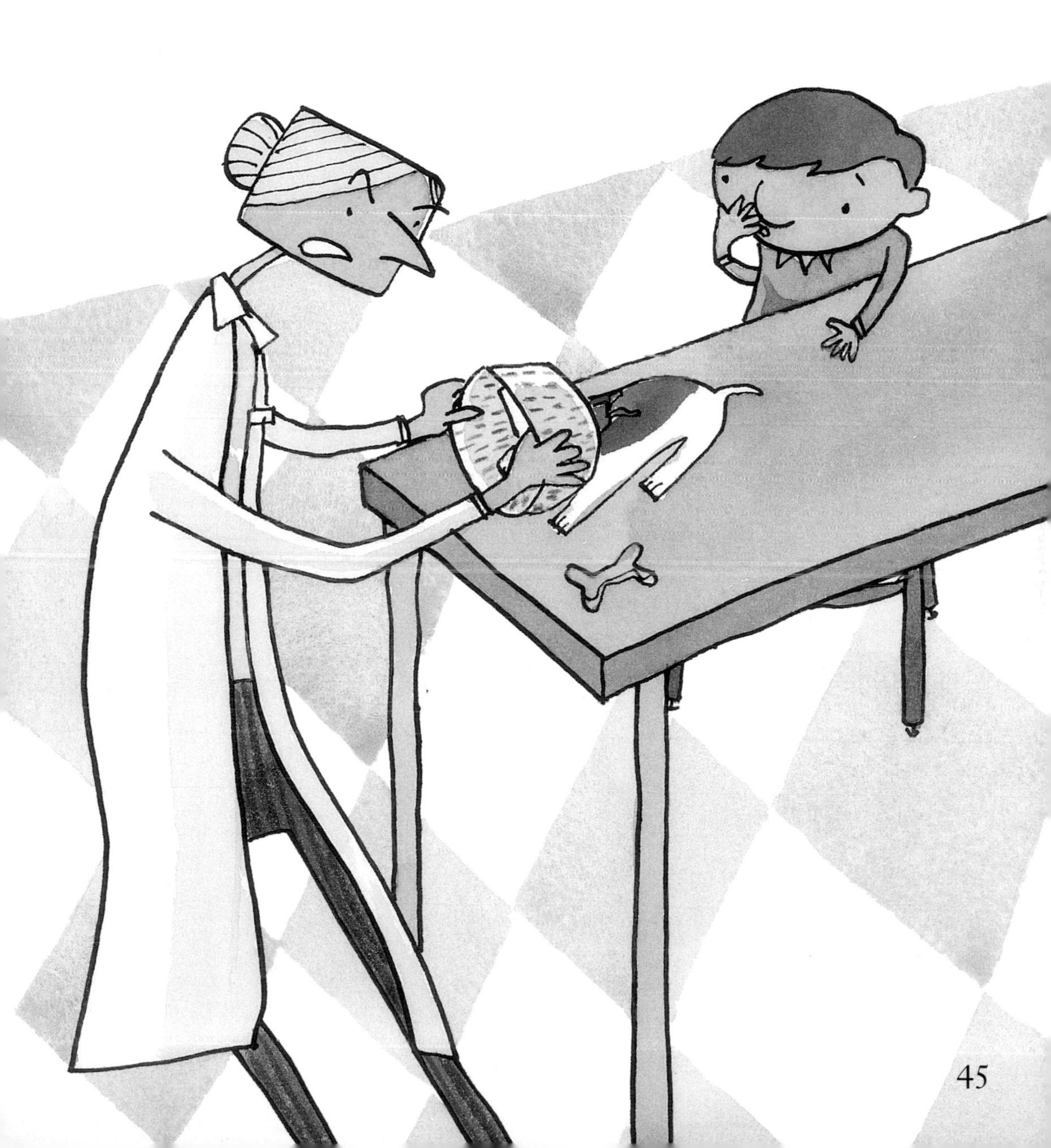

She runs

and jumps.

She circles my legs.

We play chase till it gets dark.